A NOTE TO PARENTS

When your children are ready to "step into reading," giving them the right books is as crucial as giving them the right food to eat. **Step into Reading Books** present exciting stories and information reinforced with lively, colorful illustrations that make learning to read fun, satisfying, and worthwhile. They are priced so that acquiring an entire library of them is affordable. And they are beginning readers with a difference—they're written on five levels.

Early Step into Reading Books are designed for brand-new readers, with large type and only one or two lines of very simple text per page. **Step 1 Books** feature the same easy-to-read type as the Early Step into Reading Books, but with more words per page. **Step 2 Books** are both longer and slightly more difficult, while **Step 3 Books** introduce readers to paragraphs and fully developed plot lines. **Step 4 Books** offer exciting nonfiction for the increasingly independent reader.

The grade levels assigned to the five steps—preschool through kindergarten for the Early Books, preschool through grade 1 for Step 1, grades 1 through 3 for Step 2, grades 2 through 3 for Step 3, and grades 2 through 4 for Step 4—are intended only as guides. Some children move through all five steps very rapidly; others climb the steps over a period of several years. Either way, these books will help your child "step into reading" in style!

This is how you say
the hard words in this book:

dreidel: DRAY-dul

Hanukkah: HAH-nuh-kuh

latkes: LOT-kuhs

Maccabee: MAK-uh-bee

menorah: muh-NOR-uh

miracle: MEER-uh-kul

For Amanda and Ian,
who can't wait for Hanukkah!
—N.K.

To Rosie and her Readers
—D.D.-R.

Text copyright © 2000 by Nancy Krulik. Illustrations copyright © 2000 by DyAnne DiSalvo-Ryan. All rights reserved under International and Pan-American Copyright Conventions. Published in the United States by Random House, Inc., New York, and simultaneously in Canada by Random House of Canada Limited, Toronto.

www.randomhouse.com/kids

Library of Congress Cataloging-in-Publication Data
Krulik, Nancy E. Is it Hanukkah yet? / by Nancy Krulik ; illustrated by DyAnne DiSalvo-Ryan.
  p. cm. — (Step into reading. A step 1 book) SUMMARY: A little girl waits with great anticipation all day until the sun sets and Hanukkah can begin.
ISBN 0-375-80286-X (pbk.) — ISBN 0-375-90286-4 (lib. bdg.)
[1. Hanukkah—Fiction.] I. DiSalvo-Ryan, DyAnne, ill. II. Title. III. Step into reading. Step 1 book.
PZ7.K944 Is 2000 [E]—dc21 99-044517

Printed in the United States of America July 2000 10 9 8 7 6 5 4 3 2 1

STEP INTO READING, RANDOM HOUSE, and the Random House colophon are registered trademarks and the Step into Reading colophon is a trademark of Random House, Inc.

Step into Reading®

Is It Hanukkah Yet?

A Step 1 Book

By Nancy Krulik

Illustrated by DyAnne DiSalvo-Ryan

Random House 🏠 New York

Today is Hanukkah!
I can't wait to
light the candles
and play games.

"Not yet,"
says Mommy.
"We have to wait
for the sun
to set."

Waiting is hard!
While we wait,
we polish
the menorah.

Hanukkah lasts
for eight nights.
We light one candle
for each night.

Today, I put
two candles
in place.
One candle
is for the
first night of
Hanukkah.
The second candle
lights the first one.

Mommy makes
potato pancakes.
We call them latkes.
I can't wait
to eat one!

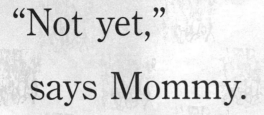

"Not yet,"
says Mommy.
"We have to wait
for the sun
to set."

Mommy tells me
the story of the
Hanukkah miracle.
The Maccabees
only had oil
to light their menorah
for one day.
But the oil lasted
for eight days!

Ding-dong.

The doorbell rings.

I run to the door.

It's Grandma
and Grandpa!

It must be Hanukkah now!

"Not yet,"
says Grandma.

"We have to wait
for the sun to set."

Grandpa hands me
a bag of
chocolate coins.
They are called gelt.
"You can eat
these now,"
he says.
I gobble the gelt.

The door opens.

Daddy is home!

I look outside.

It is dark.

"The sun has set!"
I shout.
"Is it Hanukkah
yet?"
Daddy gives me
a great big hug.
"It sure is!"
he says.

No more waiting!

Mommy lights
the candles.
I help say
the prayers.

We play
the dreidel game.
Whee!
All the candy
is for me!

We sing a song
about a dreidel.

Grandma
gives me a gift.

Wow!

It is the music box

we play with

at her house.

"Happy Hanukkah!"
Grandma says.
"Now you can
hear our song
anytime you like."

During supper,
Daddy eats
lots of latkes.
He likes
Hanukkah food.

Do you know
what I like best
about Hanukkah?

Hanukkah lasts
for eight days!
So I get to
do it all again.
I just have to
wait for tomorrow!